D0997195

Moby Dick

By Herman Melville

A new version of
the classic tale
by Archie Oliver

Cover Illustration: John Cooper, sga Illustration & Design
Illustrations: John Cooper, sga Illustration & Design
This adaptation: Archie Oliver
Editor: Heather Hammonds
Typesetting: Midland Typesetters, Maryborough, VIC, Australia

 Moby Dick
This adaptation published in 2004 by
Hinkler Books Pty Ltd
17–23 Redwood Drive
Dingley VIC 3172 Australia
www.hinklerbooks.com

© Hinkler Books Pty Ltd 2004

ISBN 1 7412 1550 1
Printed and bound in Australia

The Author
Herman Melville
(1819–1891)

Herman Melville was born in New York, in the United States of America. At the age of fifteen he went away to sea, taking a job as cabin boy aboard a ship bound for Liverpool, in England.

Melville quickly fell in love with the sea. In 1841 he joined a whaling ship on a voyage to the South Seas. It was a journey which he was to base much of the story of the Great White Whale, *Moby Dick*. He also joined the United States Navy. But by the mid 1840s he had left to start a writing career.

Moby Dick, Melville's masterpiece, was published in 1851. It has since been made into several films and television series.

His other works include novels such as *Billy Budd*, poems, and short stories such as the popular *Bartleby the Scrivener*.

Contents

Introduction

Oh, the rare old whale, mid storm and gale,
In his ocean home will be,
A giant in might, where might is right,
And King of the boundless sea.

Old sea song

Tales of giant whales were the stuff of folk legend in the olden days. The Sperm Whale, to which family Moby Dick belonged, was one of the largest creatures on the planet. The author of this book tells of Sperm Whales almost 90 feet long and around 90 tons in weight ... the weight of nearly a thousand men.

In the nineteenth century, whaling expeditions sometimes lasted several years. "There she blows!" was the familiar cry once whales were sighted; a reference to the whale's blowhole or spout, which is a kind of nostril.

Rowing boats, under the power of both oar and sail, would be launched from the mother ship to begin the attack with harpoons. Once killed, a whale would be towed back to the mother ship.

Whaling was a huge and profitable industry. The lure was whale oil and other precious materials that could be made into lamp oils, ointments, candles and lubricants.

Over many years, whales were hunted almost to extinction.

Today, whale hunting is banned in many countries. Oils and other products are made from different materials, and these magnificent creatures of the sea are protected.

But in times past, when there were many whales in the sea, things were very different . . .

The voyage of the Pequod

Chapter 1
Captain Ahab and Moby Dick

When the ghosts of old whaling men stir and stalk the dark lanes of old Nantucket town, people still talk of Captain Ahab and Moby Dick. They sit by roaring fires in the small cozy inns and taverns, and tell the legendary sea tale to newcomers. They shiver as they think of the Great White Whale and the furious Captain Ahab. And they huddle closer to the fires as they speak.

Ahab was a whaling captain, a famous figure on all the world's oceans. He was a prince among whalers . . . until the day Moby Dick, a monster whale, emerged from the depths and flew into the air above Ahab's boat.

The whale dropped down on the boat, smashing it to pieces and sending Ahab and his crew flying into the churning waters of the Pacific Ocean. Not content with destroying the boat, the great whale bit off Ahab's leg before disappearing.

The "dismasted" captain was rescued from the churning, wild ocean, but almost died of his wounds. When he recovered, he swore revenge on the monster of the deep.

So in 1848, he was ready to set sail from Nantucket Island, on America's eastern seaboard, determined to find and kill Moby Dick!

Chapter 2
The Spouter Inn

Call me Ismael. They know me in almost every sea port around the world. I am an old sea salt, always yearning for the loneliness and wildness of the ocean. I am tormented by an itch for things remote, forbidden seas and cannibal coasts.

There was nothing that frightened me in my younger days – until I met Captain Ahab for the first time. I had decided to try my hand at whaling and was joining a whaling ship called the *Pequod*; a vessel just about to leave Nantucket Island on a three year whaling hunt.

I reached the island late on a frozen winter's night, two days before the ship was due to sail. It was snowing and I could hardly find my way through the dark, frightening lanes of Nantucket, the main town on the island.

The town seemed deserted. At last I spotted an inn sign, lit by a flickering oil lamp. It read:

The Spouter Inn
Landlord: Peter Coffin

The name of the inn was taken from the whale's spout; its nostril or blow-hole. The landlord's name gave me little hope for a happy stay in this godforsaken place.

"Let's scrape the ice from my frosty feet," I said to myself, "and see what sort of place this Spouter Inn is."

Inside, the billowing smoke from the open fire was so thick in the room that I could not see much, except the vague outline of a huge painting hanging on one wall. On closer examination, it proved to be a picture of a great whaling ship sinking by Cape Horn.

As my eyes grew accustomed to the smoke, I saw that the walls were also lined with old whaling harpoons. Some had little signs placed beside them.

"With this harpoon," read one, *"did Nathan Swain kill fifteen whales between sunrise and sunset."*

Now I began to make out a few faces in the darkness; sailors all drinking a rum or two. And serving them was a withered and weathered old seadog, the landlord himself.

The Spouter Inn

I spotted an inn sign.

"And what are you after, master?" asked Coffin.

"A bed for the night," said I.

"We've none left," he replied. "Yet, you could share a bed with someone. You ain't got any objections to sharin' a blanket with a harpooner, have you? I suppose you're goin' a whalin', so you'd better get used to sharin'. The cabins on them ships are awful crowded."

I had no choice. "Who's my bedmate?" I asked.

"A harpooner who eats nothin' but blood-red steaks," he answered, a strange grin crossing his face. "Some say he was once a cannibal."

The thought of sharing a room with a cannibal chilled me more than the snow outside. But I had no choice. I took the room.

That evening, sitting close to the fire in the bar, I got talking to some of the whaling men already there. I mentioned that I was to sail on the *Pequod*.

"Have you clapped eyes on Ahab yet?" one sailor asked.

"Who's Ahab?" I said.

"You're new to this game, aren't you," he replied. "Everyone in whaling knows Ahab. He's the captain of the *Pequod*. Forty years a

"And what are you after, master?"

whaling man, and a strange man indeed. You can't miss him. He's only got one leg."

"How did he lose his leg?" I asked.

"A whale stole it," he laughed. "A whale devoured it, chewed it up, crunched it to bits and spit it out! Ah ha! So it did."

The sailor wasn't finished yet. "Ahab is a mighty strange soul, especially since he lost that leg. He's got something personal against the whale that stole it. He rants and raves at that whale sometimes. He calls it Moby Dick."

The sailor came closer, as though what he wanted to say was too dangerous to be overheard. "They say it was long prophesied by a preacher-man that a whale would steal his leg."

Later, I talked with another man. When he heard I was to sail under Captain Ahab, he took me aside. "I was with him when he lost that leg to the accursed whale," he explained. "He went out of his mind for a while, but that was probably due to the shooting pains in his bleeding stump."

"Go on," I said.

"Well, he's been kind of moody ever since," he continued. "Not himself, if you know what I mean. But if you're willing and brave enough to throw a harpoon down a whale's throat, and then jump down after it, then Ahab is the captain for you."

I eventually crept off to bed. There was no sign of my bedmate. When Coffin brought me some food, I asked him where he was.

"Oh, he won't be back 'til late," he said. "He'll be out selling his heads."

"Selling his heads?" said I. "Are you joking?"

"Nope," said he. "He's a native of the South Seas, just arrived. Brought with him lots of

I talked with another man.

shriveled heads; sort of embalmed skulls. Human heads. Great curiosities round here. Sold most of them already. But I saw him go out tonight with the last four dangling around his waist. They've all got a good head of hair if you want one."

With that, Coffin left me, closing the door behind him. I shivered. The room was as cold as ice, but I shivered more at the thought of my bedmate returning with human heads rattling around his waist.

There was a huge double bed on one side of the room. I clambered into it without taking any of my clothes off. Then I lay down and prayed to heaven that I would still be alive in the morning.

I did fall asleep, but awoke again after a few hours. There were footsteps outside and flickering candle light coming under the door. The door opened and a giant figure of a man, carrying a large canvas bag, appeared. A single monstrous human head hung from his waist.

Chapter 3
Queequeg

The stranger entered the room, taking no notice of me. I lay perfectly still without saying a word. I couldn't have spoken in any case. My whole body was shaking with terror.

He put his candle down on a sideboard and placed the head beside it. The head was well preserved, with wrinkled skin and eyes that twinkled in the glow of the candle light. It was a few moments before I managed to drag my eyes away and look at the man who had brought it into the room.

What a sight! He was wearing a tall beaver-skin hat. And beneath that hat was the most extraordinary face I had ever seen. It was darkish purple in color and covered with darker looking squares.

I suddenly realized that the harpooner's face was a mass of tattoos. When he removed his hat I saw that he was bald, but his head was covered in even more tattoos. And the

The stranger entered the room.

fearsome man's teeth were shaped like shark's teeth. Each tooth had been carved to a sharp point.

I would have leapt out of bed and escaped if I could. But now he turned towards the bed and saw me. I was as much afraid of him as I would have been, had the devil himself strode into the room.

He took off his shirt and I saw that his whole body was covered with more dreadful tattoos. The next moment, he extinguished the candle and leapt into the bed. He was a huge man and I was almost bounced out of the bed and onto the floor. At last, I found my voice again. I screamed!

My own scream was immediately echoed by another – my bedmate's scream.

It would have been hard to tell who screamed the loudest.

"Landlord! Landlord!" I called out. "Save me!"

It seemed like ages, but at last Coffin's head appeared around the door. He held up his candle and looked down at his two guests. "You have nothin' to worry about," he said to me, roaring with laughter. "It's the harpooner. Your bedmate. He wouldn't harm a hair on your head."

He then introduced me. "This is Queequeg. As I told you before, some say he was once a cannibal. But he never harmed anyone as far as I know. A good Christian gentleman, is Mr. Queequeg."

Queequeg didn't speak, but gave me a big smile with his pointed teeth and shook my hand like a country gent. I have to admit that after that, I slept like a log.

I awoke the next day to find Queequeg already dressed in a thick jacket, leather trousers and shiny black boots. He nodded in a friendly way as he put his beaver-skin hat on his head. Then he reached for his harpoon, which I now saw had been hidden under the bed. He looked at it for a moment in an affectionate way. It was obviously a prized possession.

He walked over to the small basin in the room and ran a little water. With the help of some soap, he shaved himself with one of the gleaming, razor-sharp barbs on the harpoon. Then without a word, he marched out of the room.

After breakfast, I walked around the town. I found myself in a chapel. It was full of sailors and whaling men, no doubt saying a prayer to keep them safe on the next voyage. The walls

It was a prized possession.

15

of the chapel were covered in memorial stones for lost whalers. One read:

Sacred to the memory of Robert Long,
Willis Ellery, Nathan Coleman, Samuel Canny,
Seth Macey and Samuel Gleig
Of the whaling Ship Eliza
Who were all towed away out of sight by a
whale in the Pacific Ocean on December 31,
1839

I noticed Queequeg in the congregation. He was saying his prayers. Just then, the chapel minister climbed into the pulpit. The actual pulpit was shaped like a ship's bow, and a swinging rope ladder was the only way to reach it.

From that pulpit, he read the story of Jonah who was swallowed by a whale.

Queequeg and I walked back to the Spouter Inn together. Again he didn't talk, but he seemed to be happy in my company. Afterwards, he gave me a present – his last shriveled head!

I didn't want to offend Queequeg, but I managed to persuade the local barber to take the head in exchange for a haircut and a shave.

Chapter 4
Aboard the Pequod

On Christmas Eve, the night of our departure, Queequeg and I were walking down to the ship when a stranger suddenly appeared out of the shadows.

"Are you sailing in that ship?" he asked.

"What ship?" said I.

"That there," he replied, pointing to the *Pequod*, which was moored close by.

"Aye," I answered. "We have signed for a three year whaling voyage."

"Perhaps you signed away your lives as well," said the stranger.

"What are you jabbering about?" I asked.

"You're going with Ahab, aren't you?" said the man.

"What's it to you?" I replied, becoming rather annoyed at the man.

"I sailed with him once, but never again," he said. "I saw him lose his leg. No man suffered more. No whale will suffer more when Ahab finds the creature that did it."

"What's your business here?" I asked.

"Some say I am a prophet," he answered with a frightening gleam in his eyes. "They say I prophesied he would lose his leg. That prophecy came true. Now, so they say, I have made another prophecy. That the whale will eat the rest of old Ahab this time. Are you still ready to go with him?"

"You're talking gibberish, man," I said, with a stern frown.

"You may say that," the man replied, "but beware of old Fedallah, a mystic from the east. You'll meet him one day. He's the only man who can frighten Ahab. Now I must be gone. I suppose there's no good I can do here now. If you've signed to join the ship, what's signed is signed, and what's to be will be."

"Now look here," I interrupted. "If you've got anything important to tell us, then out with it now."

"I've said all that's needed," replied the man. "Now I'll be saying good evening to you. I don't expect I'll see you again, unless it's in heaven on Judgment Day."

The stranger slid away into the darkness. Out of the dark I heard his last words. "Oh by

"You're going with Ahab, aren't you?"

the way, they call me Elijah."

Neither Queequeg nor I answered the man. We continued on to the ship, where other members of the crew were boarding. There was no sign of Captain Ahab then, or when the ship slipped anchor at ten o'clock that evening.

Soon we were free of the land. Our three year voyage was underway. The *Pequod* was an old, rather small three-masted vessel. Her ancient decks were worn and cracked. She had a helmsman's tiller carved out of one great piece of whale bone.

Between the foremast and mainmast was a brick kiln and chimney. It had furnaces beneath it and two great iron melting pots on top. These were used to produce the oil from the whale's blubber, or fat. The sails above the kiln were already heavily stained with soot.

There was still no sign of Captain Ahab but Mr. Starbuck, the ship's First Officer, explained why he was not on deck. "The captain's still abed," he informed us. "He's sort of sick, yet he doesn't look sick. He's a very strange man these days, is Captain Ahab."

It was a cold and cheerless Christmas Eve we spent, as we slowly glided out into the Atlantic Ocean. The misty, damp night chilled

Our voyage was underway.

our bones. A screaming gull, no doubt lost in the darkness above, flew overhead. The ship began to roll in the swell, as we committed our fate to the oceans.

Chapter 5
Captain Ahab

I soon got to know most of the crew quite well. We settled into a routine as the northern ice and freezing weather gave way to warmer seas, as we headed south.

Each day started with lookouts scurrying up to the tops of the three masts, or mastheads, as they were known. From here, all day long and for as long as light remained in the sky, they kept a sharp lookout for the first sighting of any whales.

From those high points, far above the ocean and tossed by the sea, novice sailors felt as relaxed as if they were standing on a bull's horns. And in the chill blasts of winter gales, masthead men could die of cold, or worse, be sent tumbling to their deaths.

Yet on warmer, quiet days, the view was so spectacular that I would often join Queequeg when he was on duty at the masthead. Queequeg, I discovered, was one of three harpooners on the ship. The other two were Tashtego and Daggoo.

Tashtego was an American Indian, from Martha's Vineyard in Massachusetts. His family and his ancestors had worked in the whaling business for centuries. Tashtego had a reputation as a fearless and brave hunter.

Daggoo was an African. He was six feet and five inches in his socks. Suspended from his ears were two great golden rings. As a boy, he had joined a whaling ship in his native Africa and never returned home. He was said to be the sharpest whaling marksman on the ocean.

The three harpooners spent much of their time up on the mastheads.

After three days at sea, there was still no sign of the captain. I wondered if we were ever to see him. Then one morning I came up to see a man standing on the quarter deck. The figure filled me with a terrible sense of foreboding. It had to be Captain Ahab.

He sent shivers running up and down my spine. Physically, he was tall and broad. He looked as if he was built of solid bronze. His face was well-scorched by years on the oceans. A great livid white scar stretched from his right cheek all the way down to the base of his neck.

The three harpooners.

Whether it was left by a wound or an accident at sea, I could not tell. A large hat shaded his eyes.

So powerful was the whole grim look of Ahab that for a few moments I did not notice the horrific white leg on which he partly stood. It had been carved from the bone of a long-dead whale.

I was struck by the captain's posture. Two holes, one on each side of the steering helm, had been drilled into the deck. And, depending on which side of the helm he was standing, he

Captain Ahab

planted his whalebone leg into one of the holes to steady himself.

But he didn't stay in any one position for long. He continually paced the deck, a distant expression on his face. At night he stalked the ship, the ghostly knocking of his whalebone leg echoing through the rigging.

Occasionally he sat down on an ancient chair by the helm. It was also made of whalebone. When he was sitting in the chair, you couldn't observe him without thinking how much he looked like an unhappy king.

Then one evening, Ahab's powerful voice rang out. "Muster! Muster! Everyone on deck!"

In a few moments, we had all come up on deck. The captain was looking excited.

"What do you do when you see a whale?" he asked first.

"Sing out! Sing out a warning!" echoed some of the crew.

"And what's the song you sing then?" boomed Ahab.

"A song to the death of the whale," came the answer.

Ahab seemed cheered by the men's responses.

He raised his right hand and then drew out a bag of gold from his pocket with his left. "Some of you may have heard of the Great White Whale with its white head, wrinkled brow, speckled sides and crooked jaw. This bag of gold is for the man who finds that whale for me. So be on the lookout for him. Watch for white water. If you see so much as a bubble, sing out loud!"

To my surprise, Queequeg called out to the captain. "Captain Ahab, that Great White Whale you talk of, is it the same one that some call Moby Dick? Is it the one that stole your leg?"

"Moby Dick!" roared the captain, his eyes flaming red. "Do you know this whale?"

"Does he flick his tail in a strange way when he dives?" asked Queequeg. "Has he a curious blow-hole? Does he have the remains of ancient harpoons rusting in his sides? Does he rise up and split hunting boats in two?"

"Death and devils!" cried Ahab. "You know the beast. You have described him true. Have you seen him?"

"I have not seen him yet," replied Queequeg. "But I have heard of him. Was this truly the whale called Moby Dick?"

"Aye," said Ahab. "It was Moby Dick. He

dismasted me. He reduced me to this dread stump I stand on now. It was that accursed whale that stole my leg."

"And was it prophesied that you would lose that leg?" continued Queequeg.

"Aye, so they say," nodded Ahab. "It was Moby Dick that fulfilled the prophecy, but I have a prophecy for him now. I will chase him all the way from Africa to Australia, and New Zealand to South America, to capture him. And that is why I have gathered you together, men. Your job is to chase that whale until he spouts black blood and pays for taking my leg. Vengeance shall be mine!"

Mr. Starbuck, the First Officer, was standing beside me. "The captain worries me," I heard him say to Mr. Stubb, the Second Officer. "What good is there in seeking vengeance against a dumb creature? The man's mad."

But Ahab hadn't finished. He produced a bottle of rum and summoned his officers to drink a toast to the capture and death of Moby Dick. First, he made Starbuck drink a toast, and then Stubb and, finally, Flask, the Third Officer. Then he gave a tot of rum to each of his crew and made them swear to hunt Moby Dick to the death.

"Vengance shall be mine!"

Lastly, he beckoned to his three harpooners, Queequeg, Tashtego and Daggoo, and made them drink a toast too. "Drink to the death of Moby Dick," he said. "And beg to be drowned if we don't catch that monster of the deep!"

Queequeg, Daggoo and Tashtego willingly drank the toast. The whole crew, apart from Mr. Starbuck, seemed to be incapable of resisting the captain's calls.

To all of us, the object of Ahab's hatred had already ceased to be an ordinary, mortal whale. Now we were to hunt some god-like creature with unearthly powers.

Captain Ahab had invested Moby Dick with a terror unimagined, that day.

Chapter 6
"There She Blows!"

Over the next few days I learned more about Moby Dick from other members of the crew. Superstition surrounding the whale was rife. It was said that many sea captains had seen him and many legends had grown up around the beast. There had been sightings in all the southern seas.

One of the whale's most frightening abilities, they said, was his cleverness as an actor. One moment he would be pretending to flee and the next, turning on his pursuers. He would then chase the hunters all the way back to the mother ship, and give the ship a great wallop in the process.

Of late, there had been tales of the great beast attacking more ships. He had already taken several lives. Those who had seen Moby Dick close up and survived could only meekly utter their terror at the sight of the ocean giant.

There were several documented stories of

such attacks, that had appeared in newspapers at the time. One whaling captain had been cruising in the Pacific Ocean when he spotted a shoal, or pod, of Sperm Whales. He launched his whaleboats, taking command of one himself, and gave chase.

Suddenly, from the middle of the shoal, came a huge whale with many a white shade and mark upon him. He bore down directly on the mother ship and used his forehead as a battering ram.

Moby Dick, for it surely was he, created a huge hole in the ship's hull. The ship sank within ten minutes, with the loss of everyone aboard except the hunters in its whaleboats.

The same captain was attacked again the following year, in a new boat. Once more it was the Great White Whale that breached the ship's side.

An American warship also came to grief at the hands of Moby Dick. The captain swore blind that a whale, even of Moby Dick's size, could do a warship no damage. The next day, however, the Great White Whale struck again, creating a huge gash in the ship's side.

The captain only just managed to reach shore in time, before his ship sank.

Using his forehead as a battering ram.

The creature's strength seemed to be matched only by its malice towards the human hunters.

So the challenge was set. The men of the *Pequod* seemed as bold a group of men as ever sailed the oceans. Or was it that they were terrified of what Captain Ahab might do to them if they didn't join his hunt?

Every minute of the day he would call up to the lookouts on the mastheads. "Keep your eyes open! He's out there somewhere."

Some said that Ahab was setting out on a hopeless task to find a single whale among the world's vast oceans. But that wasn't the way Ahab saw it. He had sailed the oceans for so many years that he knew all the tides and currents of each one.

He could calculate where the White Whale and his brothers and sisters would find their food at any particular time of the year. He knew where and when the giant beasts would find the tastiest delicacies. In other words, Captain Ahab understood whales more than most members of his own race.

***

"Keep your eyes open!"

"There She Blows!"

One warm afternoon Tashtego and Daggoo were at the mastheads, holding on tightly as the ship swayed from side to side in the gentle swell, a movement greatly exaggerated at the very top of the masts.

Suddenly, I saw Tashtego's right arm shoot forward, pointing. It seemed ages before his words reached all the way down to the deck. "There she blows! There! There she blows!"

Next I heard Ahab's voice. It sounded like a desperate scream. "Where? Where does she blow?"

"Two miles off the starboard bow," cried Tashtego, still pointing. "A shoal of whales."

"Prepare the boats," shouted Ahab.

A team of seamen rushed to the side of the ship and unhooked the chains holding three boats and three cranes.

The hunting crews of the *Pequod* were an unusual mix. Mr. Starbuck was in charge of Boat Number One. Just thirty years old, he had faced a thousand perils on the world's oceans already. A Nantucket man, his hard-baked skin gave evidence of many years at sea.

Starbuck was a man of action, loyal to his skipper and brave in the face of danger. "I'll have no man aboard who is *not* afraid of a whale," he used to say. "A fearless man is more dangerous than a coward."

Each boat carried its own harpooner. Starbuck's man was the experienced harpooner Queequeg.

Boat Number Two was led by the Second Officer, Mr. Stubb. A native of Cape Cod, he was a happy-go-lucky soul, neither excessively brave nor a coward. He was prepared for any perils that might come.

Some said Stubb ran his boat as if he had asked his harpooner and oarsmen to come to a pleasant dinner rather than a deadly encounter. To him, the jaws of death had become a very comfortable chair. Stubb's harpooner was the brave Tashtego, from Martha's Vineyard.

Boat Number Three was under the captaincy of the Third Officer, Mr. Flask. He was another native of Martha's Vineyard. A short, stocky man, it was said that he saw the whale hunt as a very personal battle. There wasn't room on the ocean for both Flask and the whale. Flask's harpooner was the skilful Daggoo.

I saw Tashtego and Daggoo leave the masthead and clamber down to the deck. Grabbing

Preparing the boats.

their harpoons, they leapt into the whale boats. I took my place with Queequeg in Starbuck's boat.

"Lower away," ordered Ahab.

The three boats dropped away into the sea below. The oars splashed. The boats were now in pursuit.

Suddenly, I saw a fourth boat drop from a crane near the front of the ship. It was Ahab. He was standing at the back of his boat. His crew was made up of a powerful squad of rowers and a mysterious man who I later found out was Fedallah; an Indian mystic who advised Ahab on the day to day omens of the voyage.

Fedallah was the mystic that Queequeg and I had been warned about, the night we set sail . . .

Chapter 7
A Stormy Hunt

"Spread yourselves out!" roared Ahab. "Starbuck, stay in the center. Stubb, move out right. Flask to the left."

Ahab was issuing orders as one of the whales blew again from its blowhole, sending a jet of water and steam into the air.

"There she blows!" bellowed Ahab into the wind.

"Pull away, lads," cried Starbuck.

"Heave ho, my boys," shouted Stubb.

"Whales ahead, my lucky chums," said Flask. "Remember the bag of gold for the White Whale, if he's among them."

But a few moments later, the whales disappeared beneath the waves.

Ahab raised his arm. It was the signal to stop. All four boats came to a halt. There was complete silence as each man looked down into the water beneath them. Most instinctively knew that the whales were now directly below them.

Ahab was issuing orders.

Breathless and still, Ahab and his men waited. Starbuck, Stubb and Flask were standing at the back of their boats, balancing themselves as each ocean swell came silently through. Waiting. Waiting. Waiting. The tension was unbearable.

To a landlubber, there would have been no clue to the whereabouts of any whale. But each man afloat that day knew the whales were close. So very close.

Suddenly, Flask shouted, "Here they come, boys!"

The first whale broke the surface, its swishing tail narrowly missing Stubb's boat. One by one, the others followed. No boats were hit, but the water was turned into a white maelstrom of froth and foam.

"After them!" roared Ahab.

Just then, the weather began to change and a squall blew in. The wind was getting up and the boats were swaying this way and that.

"Stand up, Mr. Queequeg," ordered Starbuck. "Prepare your harpoon."

Queequeg, harpoon in hand, sprang to his feet.

"There!" yelled Starbuck, pointing to an area of boiling white water. "Let him have it!"

Queequeg's right arm drew back as far as it would go and then shot forward with a long follow-through. The harpoon flew like lightning. Behind it flashed the rope line that attached it to the boat.

The whale instinctively flipped its tail and turned. The harpoon bounced off the creature's back. Queequeg cursed.

At that moment, the boat hit an incoming wave. Queequeg was thrown back into his seat. The boat rocked in the air and crashed to the surface with the sound of thunder.

The little vessel was swamped. The squall had turned into a storm. The wind had turned from a breeze to a howl. We called out to the other boats, but they were now hidden by the ever-rising waves.

Still we rowed in the direction in which the whale had vanished, as Queequeg hauled his harpoon in. The harpoon rope was neatly coiled again and all eyes peered through the storm, looking for any sight of the whales returning.

After a while we realized it was hopeless. Soaking wet and shivering with cold, we just waited for the storm to calm. The whales were now long gone. Night fell. We called out again

The little vessel was swamped.

and again, but got no answer from any of the other crews.

We were alone in the storm. It was the longest night of my life. As dawn finally arrived and the waves began to lessen, we looked around us. The ocean seemed completely empty. Then, suddenly, we saw a moving speck. In the distance was the *Pequod.* She had found us and we were safe.

Queequeg and I were the last to be hauled aboard our mother ship.

"Queequeg," I said, "is life as a whaler always this dangerous?"

"All the time, Mr. Ismael," he replied. "The best whalers will always lower their boats in a gale if there's a whale to be caught."

Later that morning I heard Ahab muttering to himself. "No sign of Moby Dick today, but I shall have him!"

Chapter 8
The Midnight Whale

The next few weeks in the South Atlantic Ocean passed with no sightings of any whales. Now we headed eastward towards the Cape of Good Hope, on the southern tip of Africa.

One evening I saw Fedallah, Ahab's mystic, come on deck. Now, I don't think I had ever seen him on deck before. Why should he come that night? He hadn't seen me, so I watched him closely.

He walked slowly to the main mast and clambered up to one of the sail spars – a wooden cross beam secured to the mast. Fedallah sat down on the spar, supporting himself by holding onto one of the sail ropes. He began to stare out across the water.

It was a warm night, with a full moon shining. Despite being almost at the top of the mast, I could see Fedallah quite clearly. Suddenly, he raised his right arm, and in complete silence, pointed to the spot on the horizon that he seemed to have been staring at. Immediately, I spotted a flash of reflected light in that area.

For almost two hours, Fedallah stared out in the same direction. The flash of light came and went several times as he watched the sea.

I heard the ship's bell sound the midnight hour. At that moment Ahab appeared on deck with his telescope. He scanned the horizon. He didn't say a word for some time, but when his eye reached the place that Fedallah had been staring at, he cried out immediately.

"There she blows!"

In a few moments, most of the crew was all up on deck again. Ahab didn't call for the boats to be launched because we were too far off.

I showed Stubb where I had seen the reflected light in the distance. He took out his telescope and looked through it briefly, before handing it to me. I looked out. To my extreme surprise, I saw what that light had been. It was a ghostly jet of water gleaming in the moonlight. It was a whale blowing through its blow-hole.

Captain Ahab instructed the helmsman to turn the ship towards the spot and ordered all sails to be raised. He was planning a night chase in the moonlight!

Suddenly, he raised his right arm.

It was a dangerous business to launch the boats at night, but Ahab wasn't going to miss any chances. As soon as the ship sailed close enough, three boats were launched. But we had seen our last of that jet. Along with its owner, it had vanished. There wasn't a whale to be seen.

We wearily returned to the ship. I saw that Fedallah was still sitting high up on the spar. Had he used his magic to conjure up Moby Dick? I wondered about that.

The weather was clear the next day and that evening Ahab ordered that all the mastheads should be manned through the night.

The Midnight Whale, as the creature had quickly become known, reappeared in the moonlight. But again it vanished, as soon as the boats were launched. Night after night the whale appeared at midnight, only to disappear shortly afterwards. Fedallah never left his seat on the spar, day or night.

The whale spooked all of us, Ahab included. Most of the crew was convinced that it was Moby Dick. The moon always seemed to highlight a bright patch on the whale's head. The mysterious creature didn't stay in the same position, either. It seemed to be beckoning us

The whale spooked all of us.

on, ever-south and into more remote seas.

We were becoming very superstitious, especially when the winds of the Cape of Good Hope began to howl around us and sea ravens lined up on our bow; a sure sign of approaching danger.

Captain Ahab now seldom left the deck at night, and sometimes he joined Fedallah in the rigging. There, they talked long into the night. I got the impression that the Midnight Whale was beginning to haunt both of them.

Night after night the whale's jet could be seen at midnight. Yet we never got any closer to that phantom creature.

Chapter 9
First Blood

After rounding the Cape of Good Hope and pushing north-east into the Indian Ocean, the Midnight Whale was seen no more.

The weather grew warm and I enjoyed being up at the masthead with Queequeg whenever I could. One day I was with him while the rest of the crew was dozing below. I was rather sleepy myself from the heat of the day and the gentle rocking motion of the boat.

I became aware of an area of disturbed water some way off. Then I saw bubbles surfacing closer to the ship. I was instantly wide awake. Not more than 250 yards away was a gigantic Sperm Whale. It was rolling in the warm waters like a capsized hull, its broad, glossy back glistening in the sun's rays.

Queequeg and I roared out as one, "There she blows!"

"Launch the boats," ordered Ahab.

I watched as they dropped into the water

"There she blows!"

with their crews. The whale immediately took off at speed.

Stubb's boat was nearest. I saw Tashtego grab his harpoon.

"Watch him, Tashtego," I heard Stubb call out. "Take it slowly."

Now it was a race. Mr. Starbuck with Queequeg and Mr. Flask with Daggoo were both trying to catch up. Captain Ahab and his team of rowers weren't far behind.

The officers called on the oarsmen for more power. Then Stubb gave the first command to launch the attack. "Stand up, Tashtego!"

Tashtego was up in a flash. Almost as quickly, he hurled his harpoon. The distance between the boat and the whale was about forty feet. The rope unraveled like a whirling snake.

The harpoon struck its target and four men took hold of the rope.

"Haul her in!" cried Stubb.

But now the whale tried to escape. It was a strong animal and continually made headway. Each time it did, the rope raced through the men's hands, burning them badly. Great jets of steam and water shot from the creature's blow-hole, and blood poured from its side. Tashtego released another deadly harpoon.

The whale was weakening.

"Pull in! Pull in!" screamed Stubb. "We have him now!"

The end came quickly. The whale suddenly stopped pulling the boat. It was dead. Its heart must have burst. The hunt was over.

The whale's dead body was floated back to the *Pequod* and chained alongside the hull. The next two days were spent butchering the creature, and cooking the blubber and flesh to retrieve the oils, greases and waxes that would be sold for a handsome price.

Hurling his harpoon.

The victim also provided us with some fresh meat. Whale steaks were a welcome change for the crew.

How odd, I thought, that the ship's own lamps were powered by whale oil. We were enjoying a meal of whale meat, an occasion lit by the oils provided by the same creature.

The next day, what remained of the whale was to be released from the chains and allowed to float away. The beast was now just a skeleton. Captain Ahab and all the crew were on deck to see it go, as Tashtego clambered onto the skeleton to untie the chains.

We all saw the huge underwater shadow that now suddenly appeared close to the ship. A giant whale exploded through the surface and into the air above us.

It was a huge Sperm Whale. At it began to fall back towards the water, it flicked its tail violently, catching poor Tashtego on the back of the dead whale. He was thrown high into the air. At last, he began to descend, falling into the sea some fifty yards from our ship. He vanished beneath the waves.

"Man overboard!" cried the captain.

There was no time to launch one of the small whaling boats. Besides, we were sure that

It was a huge Sperm Whale.

Tashtego must already be dead. Then I saw a figure flying through the air above me. Queequeg had dived off a mast spar and now sliced through the water. He swam furiously to the spot where Tashtego had last been seen, and dived under the water.

Time stood still. We waited. More than a minute passed. No man could hold his breath under water this long! Suddenly, the surface was broken again and Queequeg emerged with Tashtego in his arms.

We hauled the pair aboard and pumped the water out of Tashtego. With a cough and a splutter, he finally regained consciousness.

Now, at last, we had a moment to think clearly. Captain Ahab spoke for us all. "Curses on the beast – that was Moby Dick!" he snarled angrily.

Chapter 10
A Meeting at Sea

We killed several whales in the days that followed. Yet, there was no further sign of Moby Dick, or the Midnight Whale for that matter. If the whales were haunting us, so was Fedallah. He rarely came down from his high perch in the rigging, unless it was to ride out on Ahab's boat.

"He'll bring no good to the *Pequod*," Stubb said to me one day. "If I saw him standing by the side of the ship and no one was looking, I'd gladly push him overboard. He's the devil in disguise."

"Why does Ahab keep so close to him?" I asked.

"They say he has the power of prophecy," replied Stubb. "Perhaps Ahab is just frightened of him. Perhaps he thinks Fedallah will charm Moby Dick to jump into the boat."

Our conversation was interrupted by a shout from the masthead. "Sail-ho!" cried Daggoo.

A ship was approaching. It was a whaler

A ship was approaching.

which turned out to be the *Samuel Enderby*, from London.

Captain Ahab ordered all sails to be taken down and his boat launched. He wanted to talk with the captain of the other ship. I was one of the crew who went with him. Poor Ahab had great difficulty getting aboard the *Samuel Enderby*. In the end, he slipped, cracked his leg and had to be dragged aboard.

Our one-legged captain was surprised to find himself face-to-face with a one-armed captain. Captain Mounttop, skipper of the *Samuel Enderby*, wore a false whalebone arm.

"Let us shake whalebones together," said Ahab. "You have an arm that can never bend, and I a leg that will never run again. Tell me, was it the work of the White Whale? Did Moby Dick take your arm?"

"It was that brute indeed," replied Captain Mounttop.

"And how did Moby Dick introduce himself to you? What happened?"

"I don't know exactly," said the English captain. "I was in one of our whaling boats when a harpoon was thrown at the largest creature we had ever seen. He must have got his teeth caught on the harpoon rope and he was furiously snapping at the line. All I can remember is seeing the beast leap high in the air above me. Then I was knocked unconscious. When I opened my eyes again, I found I was an arm short. The whale's teeth had cut it clean off, like a guillotine."

"What happened to the White Whale?" Ahab inquired eagerly. "What became of him?"

"We saw him at least twice more," said Captain Mounttop.

"Did you launch the boats after him?" asked Ahab. "Did you attack him? Did you kill him?"

"By Jove, we didn't!" exclaimed Mounttop. "Didn't want to! Losing one arm was enough. No more white whales for me. No doubt there would be great glory to be had in killing him. I know that. And the creature would have had a huge load of oil inside him. Yet, he will have no more of me. And looking at your whalebone leg, Captain Ahab, I think you should do the same."

"Ye gods of the sea!" cried Ahab. "You had a chance of killing Moby Dick and you didn't take it. Which way was Moby Dick heading when you last saw him?"

"North West, towards the island of Java," answered the captain.

"Which way was Moby Dick heading?"

"Then that's where we shall go," said Ahab. "The beast won't escape me, even if I do have to give him my other leg in exchange for his life."

Ahab returned to his ship. Soon after, he planted his whalebone leg in its usual pivot hole, with disastrous results.

The leg, badly damaged by his hard landing on the *Samuel Enderby*, suddenly split from top to bottom. Ahab screamed with pain as it cut into his hip.

"Curses!" he cried. "Moby Dick, you'll pay for this!"

The threat echoed across the water to where the *Samuel Enderby* was just raising sail and about to sail on.

"You're mad, Captain Ahab," shouted Captain Mounttop, through his bullhorn loud-speaker. "You'll not rest until you have your revenge on the White Whale."

Never was a truer word said.

Chapter 11
The Captain's New Leg

Captain Ahab, having seen off the *Samuel Enderby*, summoned the ship's carpenter to his cabin. "Mr. Able, make me a new leg," he demanded. "And don't waste any time in doing it. It must be ready by morning."

The fire in the ship's forge was lit for the ship's blacksmith to make the iron bolts and straps to secure the false leg. Meanwhile, Able had taken his saw to what remained of a whale's jawbone. From that one piece of bone he carved a fine leg, shaped to match Ahab's living leg.

I watched as he worked. "I hope you have the captain's measurements right," I said.

"I do," said Able. "This is not the first new leg I have made for Captain Ahab. Since first losing his leg on his last voyage, he has lived with – and broken – many other legs. He drives his false legs hard and his real leg even harder."

"Does the new leg hurt him when it's strapped to his thigh?" I asked.

The Captain's New Leg

He carved a fine leg from the jawbone.

"Not the false one," replied Able, "but a dis-masted sailor never completely loses the feeling of his real leg that once was. The memory and feeling of it is always there, and I know for a fact that it pains the captain sometimes."

***

A week later the *Pequod* reached the South China Sea, and was heading north towards the Pacific Ocean. The last few days had been stormy and Mr. Starbuck had noticed that there was a leakage of some whale oil down in the ship's storage hold. He went to see Captain Ahab.

"We'll have to stop the ship for a few days to hunt out the leaks," he said. "It might be just a few barrels. The weather's been hot and the barrel hoops may have loosened."

"What!" cried Ahab. "Stop the ship for a few days?"

"It's either that," said Starbuck, "or else lose our profit for the voyage."

"Why should I care about profit?" said Ahab. "Let the oil leak. Leaky barrels – the ship's just one large leaky barrel. I'll not stop the ship just to find those leaks."

"What will the ship's owners say?" asked

"What will the ship's owners say?"

Starbuck. "What will they say if they lose their profit from the voyage?"

"They can stand on Nantucket beach and cry to the wind for all I care," replied the captain. "The real owner of a ship is its captain. And that is me. My profit is Moby Dick's death, not a profit from the oil his relatives give me. Now be gone!"

"We must stop," insisted Starbuck.

Ahab seized a loaded musket and pointed it at Starbuck. "There is only one master on this ship and that is me," he said quietly. "So unless you want to join the whales, return to the deck and your duties at once."

Starbuck retreated through the cabin doorway. But he was still bold enough to make one last comment. "You have every reason to hate Moby Dick," he said, "but you should beware of yourself, Captain. Ahab should beware of Ahab."

With that, Starbuck was gone.

Ahab was puzzled. Why should he beware of himself? Was he not the captain? Why should he be frightened of himself?

Starbuck knew better than most that the captain had become a danger to both himself and the crew of the *Pequod*.

Chapter 12
Queequeg's Coffin

Captain Ahab had refused to stop the ship, so poor Queequeg was sent below to hunt down the leaks. It would have been a difficult job with the ship at anchor. But with the *Pequod* still rising and falling in the South China Sea, the job was highly dangerous.

After a full two days of searching, he emerged from the smelly, dark depths of the hold with his report. He had mended six barrels and the leaks had all been stopped. He also returned with a dreadful cold from working in the chill damp of the hold. It quickly turned into a raging fever.

Queequeg took to his hammock and there he lay, wheezing and sneezing, day after day. He was wasting away with the fever. The rest of the crew was sure he would die.

One morning, his head briefly cleared and he made a last request. "I saw in Nantucket," he said weakly, "how dead whalers are buried,

Queequeg returned with a dreadful cold.

not in regular coffins but in small wooden canoes. It is my last wish that I am laid to rest in just such a canoe. The carpenter will have seen these canoes before. Ask him to make me one as a last kindness to me."

Mr. Able knew well how whalers were buried. He himself had made several canoes for the purpose. He immediately promised to build one for Queequeg.

While Queequeg was drifting between life and death, Mr. Able took his measurements with great accuracy. It took the carpenter two days to build the canoe-shaped coffin, which was to carry Queequeg to the next world. When the last nail was driven home and the lid duly fitted, he carried it down to the ship's hold to await its duty.

Queequeg, still drifting in and out of his fever, demanded that the canoe coffin should be brought to his cabin immediately. He took a great interest when it arrived, calling for a harpoon to be laid inside it, as well as a paddle.

Queequeg also had some crackers and a bottle of water put aboard his deathly vessel, to satisfy him on the great journey that he was sure he would be making very soon. Finally, he asked to be laid in the canoe to try it for size and comfort. Four men struggled to lift him in. The carpenter had done a good job because the canoe fitted him perfectly.

Now, lying in the coffin, Queequeg crossed his arms over his chest and made his final request. He wanted the coffin lid placed over him. This was done and for the next few moments all was silence. Everyone thought he had died and gone to heaven already. But at last a voice was heard from inside the canoe.

"It seems to fit me very well," he said.

The men removed the lid and Queequeg asked to be laid in his hammock again, to await his last moments on earth.

"Poor Queequeg," said Daggoo. "Surely he has ended his roving days. The whales are safe from his powerful arm now."

"I am ready to go to my maker," whispered Queequeg, so weakly the words could hardly be heard.

Now the fever-ridden whaler closed his eyes and said no more. It was as if he had entered a dream.

We all expected that he had spoken his last. We retired to our own hammocks to sleep. But Queequeg wasn't finished. He had made every preparation for his leaving the world, and he

74

Taking a great interest in the coffin

was very pleased with the fit of his coffin. But that night, he suddenly rallied. By dawn, it was clear there was no need for the carpenter's canoe coffin.

"I can't go yet," were Queequeg's first words, as he opened his eyes. "I can't die because I have just remembered I have things left undone. So I have changed my mind about dying."

A puzzled Daggoo asked whether he had power over when he should or should not die.

"Most certainly," answered Queequeg without hesitation.

"I can't go yet."

In the next few days, Queequeg recovered completely and announced that he was fit enough to fight Moby Dick! His canoe coffin wasn't wasted, though. He used it as a sea-chest, emptying into it the contents of his canvas bag. Later, he spent many hours carving the lid with wonderful images of his own tattoos.

Chapter 13
The Great Harpoon

At last the *Pequod* reached the Pacific Ocean itself and the most famous Japanese whaling grounds. If the captain of the *Samuel Enderby* was to be believed, this was where he had lost his arm.

Captain Ahab stood on his deck, swiveling on his new whalebone leg and examining the horizon. He breathed in deeply and tasted the salt on the wind. Was that Moby Dick he smelt? His blood quickened as he walked the length of the ship to pay Mr. Perth, the blacksmith, a visit.

Mr. Perth was already surrounded by several members of the crew waiting for him to repair various pieces of equipment; harpoons, buckets, knives and other pieces of metalwork on the ship. They all stood aside as Ahab approached.

"Mr. Perth," he said, "I have a job for you. I want you to make me a harpoon; one so strong

The blacksmith went to work.

and heavy that ten giants couldn't break it. Something that will stick in a whale's rockiest bone if necessary. And make its shaft from twelve rods of iron, and twist them together as one. Clear your forge, I want to begin the work now!"

So while Queequeg, Daggoo and Tashtego pumped the air beneath the forge fire, the blacksmith went to work.

When the twelve rods were made, Ahab tested each one for strength and flexibility. He was happy with eleven of them, but told Perth to work on the twelfth a little longer.

When the twelfth rod was done, Ahab told Perth to stand aside while he himself welded all twelve rods together. It took a great deal of hammering and firing, but at last the twelve became one.

Then Mr. Perth took the final object from the captain. While it was still red hot, he plunged it into a barrel of cold water. Scalding steam shot up, and the water bubbled and hissed violently. All who watched took a step back, except the captain.

"Now we must make the barbs for the harpoon," he said.

With that, Captain Ahab handed Perth a

The water bubbled and hissed violently.

pile of old razors. "I have used these well. Now sharpen them again and weld them to the harpoon. They are made of the finest steel. Make them as sharp as needles. I have no need of razors any more. I shall not shave again until Moby Dick is mine."

Mr. Perth quickly put the razors into the fire and shaped them like arrows. When they had cooled, he welded them to the shaft.

The blacksmith was about to dip the finished object into his barrel of water, when Ahab cried out again. "No! Water is too ordinary to cool these precious barbs."

He turned to Queequeg, Daggoo and Tashtego. "Give me your right hands," he said, "and let me prick each one of you. I want blood enough to cool my implement of death."

The three men reluctantly allowed their hands to be pricked by the captain's new razor-sharp barbs. The blood flowed, just enough to cool them. The job was done.

Captain Ahab then chose an especially thick wooden pole to attach the harpoon to, and then called for a new coil of rope to be attached to it. A rope of two hundred feet was a long one on a whaler's harpoon, but Ahab wanted at least three hundred feet.

At last, all was done.

Captain Ahab picked up his weapon and stomped off down the deck, the sound of his whalebone leg and the harpoon pole ringing out on every plank.

Chapter 14
Fedallah's Prophecy

Captain Ahab and the *Pequod* had now traveled more than halfway around the world in their search for Moby Dick. Some of the crew was still convinced that the White Whale had been following them since the moment they left Nantucket Island, months before. Few forgot that distant, midnight spouting ghost whale in the Atlantic.

Ahab turned the ship and journeyed south again for a time. The weather became very pleasant and a mood of laziness fell over the crew. For the first time during the journey, they felt the peace and tranquility of the ocean. And during these moments of quietness, they forgot the tiger's heart that always lurks beneath the gentlest of ocean swells; the velvet paw with a terrible claw.

Only Ahab continued to stalk the decks, forever looking for signs of life out on the ocean. But the whales seemed to have vanished. No one saw one for days. But, at last, here was activity on the horizon. A ship hove into view. It was the *Bachelor*, a ship from Nantucket.

The *Bachelor* had just filled its last barrel with whale oil. The hatches covering the hold had been bolted down and the ship was heading home to America. It was covered in celebratory bunting, and the crew had decorated their hats with colored ribbon.

As the *Bachelor* came closer, the crew of the *Pequod* heard music coming from its decks. The happy sailors on the homeward-bounder were dancing and singing in celebration. Captain Ahab looked down from his place on the quarter deck. Lord and master of all he saw, he took in the whole happy scene.

He watched the ship approach with a growing and stubborn gloom. As the two ships came near – one full of jubilation for heading home, the other filled with forebodings of things to come – the two captains could not have been more contrasting.

"Come aboard! Come aboard!" cried the captain of the *Bachelor* through his bullhorn, raising a glass and a bottle in the air at the same time.

The Bachelor *was heading home.*

Captain Ahab ignored the greeting and spoke just six words. "Have you seen the White Whale?"

"No, sir," came the reply. "I have heard of him of course. But I don't believe in him for a moment. Now, sir, come aboard for a drink!"

"You are too jolly for me," replied Ahab. "Sail on. I have work to do."

So the *Bachelor* sailed on with the help of an ever-growing wind behind her. As for Ahab, he stared into the increasing wind, knowing that he would have to fight it all the way.

"Come aboard! Come aboard!"

Captain Ahab felt tired. He was also becoming more and more obsessed. The madness of Moby Dick was taking him over.

A strange thing happened after the *Bachelor* disappeared into the distance. For the next few days, the *Pequod* suddenly found lots of whales again. The crew killed four one evening, and Ahab caught one with his new harpoon.

Four of the five whales were quickly towed back to the *Pequod*, but Ahab's had been killed at some distance from the ship. It was decided to wait until morning to float it back.

As night fell, Ahab and his oarsmen moored their boat beside the dead whale to guard it from hungry sharks. They placed a lamp on the harpoon that still protruded from the side of the animal. That flickering lamp cast a troubled light on Ahab and the glossy, shimmering skin of the whale.

The mystic Fedallah was with Ahab that night. He awoke in the dawn hours and spoke with the captain. "I've had a dream," he said.

"What rubbish have you been dreaming now?" asked Ahab.

"I saw your future," said Fedallah, with a chill look on his face. "I cannot tell you how you'll die, but I can say this: you will not die

Fedallah spoke with the captain.

before you see two coffins on the sea."

"Foolish man," growled Ahab. "What chance of seeing two coffins on the ocean? I shall live forever!"

"Do not deny the prophecy," said Fedallah. "My dreams come true. You will see two coffins on the sea before you die."

A sickly smile crossed Ahab's lips. "Then such a sight will be a long time in the coming."

"It will come true," said Fedallah, "and I also dreamed that I would die before you. I will go before you as your pilot. My death will show you the way."

"Rubbish," said Ahab. "I promise you two things only. I will slay Moby Dick and I shall survive."

"Two more things I have to say to you," said Fedallah. "You will see me again after I die, and beware a piece of old rope."

"What, the gallows rope?" grunted Ahab. "That will never take me. There are no gallows on the ocean. I shall be immortal if your prophecy is true."

Both men fell silent as the pale morning sun began to rise over the Pacific Ocean.

Ahab shivered.

Chapter 15
Typhoon!

As the *Pequod* sailed further south, the equator came closer. Every noon hour, Ahab came out onto his quarter deck to take navigation readings of the sun with his instruments. He wanted to catch the precise moment when the sun told him that the ship was crossing the equator – the great line of latitude that spanned the world's girth.

The moment came at last. "Thou true and great sea mark," said Ahab, "you can show me where I am. But, God in heaven, thou high and mighty navigator, can you tell me where I'm going? Can you tell me where Moby Dick is now? For sure, from your high vantage spot, you are probably looking down on him at this very moment. These eyes of mine are now looking at your eyes; eyes that are even now looking at him."

Then Ahab did something most strange. "Why do I need to know where the equator lies?" he roared at the sun. "And why do I need my instruments?"

With that, he threw all his instruments overboard. "Curse you," he cried, as they sank beneath the waves. "What use is science to me? I can sail this ship without compasses and other instruments. I shall sail by eye from this day on."

Some of the officers and crew, including Starbuck and Stubb, saw what he had done. They feared for their captain's sanity and the safety of the ship.

Things took a turn for the worse that evening. A storm was blowing up on the horizon, but Ahab ignored the ever-blackening storm clouds and ordered all sails to be raised. Soon after, the *Pequod* was hit by a typhoon. Her sails were ripped to shreds and her masts were badly damaged. The ship was left like a skeleton to fight the typhoon head on.

When darkness fell, the sky and sea roared and split with thunder, and blazed with lightning. The electric flashes lit the ghostly masts and fluttering remnants of the sails.

Starbuck stared into the rigging, expecting further disasters with each lightning flash. Then he joined Stubb and Flask is a desperate attempt to lash the whaleboats securely to the ship's rail.

Typhoon!

Throwing his instruments overboard.

They successfully saved the three boats, but Ahab's, still hanging from a crane on the side of the ship, was caught by a great rolling sea. The boat was thrown into the air by the force of the wind. Then it hit the side of the ship with a great crash.

"It's a bad night!" shouted Stubb, above the roar of the storm.

"The sea will have its own way," replied Starbuck. "No one can fight a typhoon's wave. Come – let the typhoon sing in the rigging."

"Yes, old friend," said Stubb. "Let the storm sing out and we'll sing with it."

With that, Starbuck broke into an old sea shanty and Stubb, with most of the crew, joined in. It was their way of forgetting the terrors of the storm.

Oh! Jolly is the gale,
And a joker is the whale,
A'flourishin his tail,
Such a funny, sporty, gamy, jesty, hoky-poky
lad is the ocean, Oh!

The scud all a flyin',
That's his flip only foamin',
When he stirs in the spicin',

Typhoon!

Singing in the storm.

Such a funny, sport, gamy, jesty, hoky-poky lad is the ocean, oh!

Thunder splits the ships,
But he only smacks his lips,
A tastin' of this flip,
Such a funny, sporty, gamy, jesty, hoky-poky lad is the ocean, oh!

"Why are you singing?" asked Queequeg, emerging from his cabin.

"Because I'm not a brave man," answered Stubb. "I am a coward and I sing to keep up my spirits."

Just then the sky shook with a terrible peel of thunder, followed almost immediately by another flash of lightning. It lit a shadowy figure holding onto the mast by the quarter deck.

"Who's there?" shouted Stubb. "Show yourself!"

The figure emerged and they saw it was Ahab. There was another terrible flash, but this time the ship was hit. The tops of all three masts caught fire. Out to sea, the ship must have looked like three burning candles.

"We're sunk!" cried Stubb. "The flames will sink us."

Chapter 16
Remember the Oath

The fittest and strongest of the crew were sent aloft carrying wet blankets, to smother the blaze. None of them had ever been on top of the masts in such a terrible storm. The wind was so violent that each time the ship leaned over; its spars were almost in the water.

How they managed to put out the flames, no one ever knew. But they succeeded against all odds. A great hoorah went up from the rest of the crew.

"This is a good sign," said Starbuck. "Those masts are rooted in the ship's hold. So those three candles must mean the hold will soon be full and awash with whale oil."

Suddenly Ahab, who had overheard the remark, appeared beside them. "Maybe so," he said, "but those flames also light the way to the White Whale."

Another terrifying flash of lightning and roll of thunder seemed to energize the captain

They succeeded against all odds.

further. "I am a child of the fire," he cried to the heavens. "But it cannot consume me yet. My time to be turned into ashes has not yet come. The lightning flashes through my skull and my eyeballs are ablaze. Yet the storm will not harm me if the prophecy is true."

Another flash! This time the thunderbolt hit Ahab's newly-forged harpoon. It sparked, and then flared into a violent crimson ball.

Starbuck grasped Ahab's arm. "All is against us, Captain," he shouted. "The elements are all against us. Turn the ship around. Give the order. We must go home!"

Ahab would hear none of it. Instead, he hobbled over to the harpoon and grabbed hold of it. How it did not burn his hand to nothing, I know not. It was still in flames. He pointed the flaming implement to the skies and gave his crew a terrible warning.

"You all took the same oath as I," he snarled. "The oath was to hunt down the White Whale. That oath is as binding on you as it is on me. I am bound to that oath by my heart and mind, my soul and body and my lungs and my life. So are you!"

Later that night, the storm finally calmed a little. Stubb and Flask were talking quietly together, about Captain Ahab.

"Didn't you say once that any ship that Ahab sails in should have a special insurance policy?" said Flask. "You said that having the captain aboard was like having barrels of gunpowder in the hold."

"He is behaving very strangely indeed," replied Stubb. "He's already thrown away all his navigational instruments. He's completely obsessed with the White Whale, too. I'm beginning to think that whale only lives in his mind."

Just then the last puffs of the dying typhoon caught the remains of one of the tattered sails and blew it overboard.

"Thank the Lord the typhoon is almost done," said Flask. "It's been a nasty night, for sure."

"I fear there is worse to come for us all," replied Stubb quietly.

The rest of the night was spent clearing the ship of storm damage. New sails were brought out. By dawn, the *Pequod* almost looked like a ship again. Even the wind turned about, and now a stiff breeze was pushing the vessel on at good speed.

Starbuck went below to report to Captain Ahab. Outside Ahab's cabin, there was a locked cabinet used to store muskets. Starbuck

"He is behaving very strangely indeed."

noticed that the cabinet was open and that one gun was missing. He immediately wondered if Ahab had taken it.

"He's threatened me with a gun before," thought Starbuck. "What if he wants to murder me? He's certainly mad enough to murder anyone who crosses him now. He's made that clear enough."

Starbuck listened at the door. He could hear Ahab talking in his dreams.

"To the boats men!" he was muttering. "To the boats! Moby Dick is on the horizon. Man the boats! Sharpen your harpoons! We have the White Whale at last!"

Starbuck wondered whether the crew should make Ahab a prisoner and keep him in chains until they were safely ashore again. That would be better than giving him a chance to send everyone on board to their deaths just for the life of a single whale called Moby Dick . . .

Then Starbuck shook his head. Only a fool would try and imprison the captain. Why, tie him with ropes or chain him to the floor and he would still be more dangerous than a wounded tiger. The nearest land was hundreds of miles off and the nearest American law officer was thousands of miles away.

Starbuck decided to do nothing. He knocked at the door. There was no answer. Ahab was deeply asleep and hunting the oceans in his dreams. Starbuck returned to the main deck.

Ahab didn't come on deck until late in the afternoon. He stood apart from the crew, saying nothing for a while. Then the sun emerged from behind the clouds and he looked up at the sky. "Ha! Ha!" he cried. "My ship is now the sun's sea chariot. Drive on, my friend!"

Starbuck knocked at the door.

That night Ahab insisted that the sun had set in the east, rather than the west. Stubb tried to tell him that he was confused. "The sun most certainly sets in the west," he said.

"Nonsense!" laughed the captain. "I say it sets in the east and I don't need any navigational instruments to tell me so."

Stubb had seen Ahab in all his fatal pride. The old man was leading them all to their deaths.

Chapter 17
An Unusual Lifebuoy

The *Pequod* sailed on, turning north once more and heading ever-deeper into the Pacific whaling grounds. Sadly, the fates once more played a cruel card against the ship.

A young boy was among the regular mast-head whale spotters. Early one morning, he climbed up one of the masts to take his watch. Whether he was still half-asleep, or whether the ship was leaning over a wave, he had just reached the top of the mast when he slipped.

All heard the terrible cry and all saw the lad fall. The boy fell straight into the sea and was swallowed by the deep. The lifebuoy, an old barrel with ropes hanging from it, was dropped over the side. But no hand rose to seize it.

That boy was the first to fall victim to Captain Ahab's desperate search for Moby Dick. The accident convinced the crew more than ever that the *Pequod* was a doomed ship.

All saw the lad fall.

Something else happened that morning, too. The lifebuoy, old and battered, followed the boy to the bottom of the ocean. Starbuck and his fellow officers decided that it must be replaced.

It was Queequeg who found the solution. "My old canoe coffin," he said. "I have no need of it now and it will make a fine lifebuoy."

"The coffin will make a rather unusual lifebuoy," commented Stubb.

"Call the carpenter," said Starbuck.

Mr. Able arrived and was instructed on how he should adapt the old coffin.

"Shall I seal all the joints to make them waterproof, sir?" Able asked Starbuck.

"Yes," the First Officer replied.

"And seal down the lid?"

"Of course," Starbuck nodded. "Now be gone about your business."

Mr. Able went off to do his work. "Would that I could make a chair or a table now and again," he said to himself. "But no. I spend my life making whalebone legs for dismasted captains and coffins that I must turn into lifebuoys!"

Mr. Able mused on how he might arrange the new lifebuoy so that it could rescue the entire crew of the *Pequod*, some thirty souls.

"I know," he said, "I'll tie thirty lifelines to the coffin. Then if the ship goes down, there'll be thirty fine fellows all fighting for one coffin. And that will be a sight not often seen."

So Mr. Able went to work on Queequeg's coffin. The job was quickly done. Just as he finished, Captain Ahab came on deck and asked what he was doing.

"Making a new lifebuoy from this coffin to replace the barrel we lost," replied Mr. Able. "It was Mr. Starbuck's orders."

"You are the ship's carpenter, I know," said Ahab quietly. "But are you also its undertaker?"

"Aye, sir," answered Mr. Able. "I first made this coffin for Queequeg, but now he has no use for it."

"You're a rogue then," snapped Ahab. "One day you make whalebone legs and the next day a coffin to put them in!"

Was Ahab thinking of Fedallah's prophecy as he spoke?

"I only do as I'm told," said Mr. Able, looking puzzled.

Ahab stormed off with a final threat. "Never let me see that lifebuoy coffin again," he thundered, "unless you want to try it for size yourself."

Working on Queequeg's coffin.

Mr. Able took it to the one place where that the captain would probably never see it. He hung it from the back of the ship.

Chapter 18
News of the White Whale

The next day a large ship, the *Rachel*, came bearing down on the *Pequod*. Ahab hurried to the side of his ship and called over, using his bullhorn. "Have you seen the White Whale?"

"Aye," came the hurried reply, "and have you seen a whaleboat adrift?"

Ahab was overjoyed when he heard the first part of the sentence, but became very puzzled by the second part. "What do you mean? Have I seen a whaleboat? No I haven't. Why?"

By this time the *Rachel* had lowered sails and dropped anchor just ahead of the *Pequod*. A small boat was launched and Ahab saw the *Rachel*'s captain being rowed across. Soon he was aboard.

Ahab recognized him as Captain Gardiner, a Nantucket man. "What's happened?" he asked.

"Three of our whaleboats were busy yesterday afternoon," Captain Gardiner explained,

Ahab recognised him as Captain Gardiner.

"when our watchers on the masthead saw something terrible. My men were in hot pursuit when a whale with a whitish hump and head surfaced close to one of them. It was Moby Dick, for sure."

"At last!" cried Ahab. "The devil is close."

"The devil indeed," said the Captain Gardiner. "One moment our boat was hauling in another whale, the next Moby Dick leapt clear out of the water and landed on the boat. That was the last we saw of the whale or our boat. Will you help us in the search for our lost men?"

Stubb whispered to Flask, "When did you ever hear a captain bother about losing a few men in a whaling operation? I'll wager you that one of the missing men was a relative."

No sooner had Stubb made the comment than Captain Gardiner explained that his son was aboard the whaleboat. "He's only twelve years old. He persuaded me to give him a try. Oh, how I wish I'd never taken him to sea!"

Ahab's expression remained cold.

"Please," begged the *Rachel*'s skipper. "Let me charter your ship for two days to help search for him. I will gladly pay anything you want for her. Please. Perhaps my son is still alive out there."

At last Ahab spoke. "Be gone with you, Captain Gardiner," he began. "I will not do it. Even now I am losing time. Goodbye now. May God forgive me, but I must go. The White Whale awaits me. Mr. Starbuck, raise all sail immediately!"

He then turned and retired to his cabin, leaving Captain Gardiner astonished at the refusal of help. He turned and quickly boarded his boat, and returned to the *Rachel*.

Soon both ships were under way again, the *Rachel* zigzagging across the ocean in a desper-

"I will gladly pay anything."

ate search for a lost son. Ahab had no son aboard to lose, but he would gladly lose his complete crew to be rid of Moby Dick.

Captain Ahab hardly ever left the deck after the *Rachel* sailed away – not even at night. When he stood at his pivot, with his hat pulled down over his eyes, it was hard to tell whether he was asleep or awake. At night, the damp gathered in beads of dew on his hat and coat.

So, day after day and night after night, he stayed on deck staring out to sea. Perhaps he did doze off for a few minutes, but not for many. His life had now become one long watch. Yet there was another watcher – Fedallah. He kept his own watch on the captain while he silently perched aloft in the rigging.

In a strange, haunting way Fedallah and Ahab seemed one person, with a shared fate in life. Ahab now hardly spoke to any of his crew. But his voice was always heard each morning, as the first hint of dawn appeared on the distant horizon.

"Man the mastheads you lazy dogs!" he'd cry. "Keep your eyes peeled. What d'yer see? Look sharp! Look sharp!"

As the days passed, Ahab became increasingly distrustful of his officers and crew. He

He kept his own watch on the captain.

thought they might have seen Moby Dick but failed to raise the alarm out of fear for the creature. He decided to go aloft for himself and stayed up in the rigging for most of the day and night, watching for any sign of Moby Dick.

"Now I'll have first sighting of the White Whale," he said to himself. "And that's how it should be. The devilish fish is mine and mine alone. And I can claim my own bag of gold as the prize!"

All day he sat there, like a king or an emperor, his head turning all the while, watching, watching, watching . . .

But Ahab was also being watched by another creature. A Sea Hawk, considered unlucky by sailors, had spotted the captain and swooped down to investigate. Ahab was searching the horizon, unaware of the bird's arrival.

Suddenly, it flew high up into the bright blue sky and then dived down at a tremendous pace. With a flash of its wings and a screech, it had won its prize. The creature flew off with Ahab's hat in its beak.

Several of the crew watched the bird fly into the distance. Just as it was about to disappear from view, it dropped the hat into the ocean.

"Perhaps," said Stubb, "it's a warning for Captain Ahab. Perhaps it's telling him that another creature might swoop down on him, not for his cap, but to steal his life away."

Chapter 19
On the Scent of Moby Dick

The next day another ship came into view. It was the *Delight*, an American ship. Lying on the ship's forward deck were the remains of a whaling boat. It had been smashed to pieces. The name *Rachel* could just be made on one of the broken planks.

Everyone on board the *Pequod* knew immediately that it must have been the boat that was carrying the son of the captain of the *Rachel*. But Ahab had no interest in discovering whether the boy had been rescued or not.

As the ships closed in on each other, Ahab called out on his bullhorn, asking if anyone had seen the White Whale.

"The devil we have," came the reply from the captain of the *Delight*. "There were eight men in the broken whale boat you see, including the young son of the *Rachel's* captain. They were all killed by the White Whale. We saw it leap onto the boat and send everyone aboard to their deaths."

"Did you kill the monster?" shouted back Ahab.

"The harpoon hasn't been made yet that will kill that creature," was the answer from the *Delight.*

Ahab snatched up his own harpoon, the one that the blacksmith had made for him. "Look you here! Here in this hand I hold his death. This harpoon will be the end of the White Whale," he cried, brandishing it above his head. "Anointed in blood and hardened by lightning itself, I swear I will plant this harpoon where the White Whale most feels his accursed life."

"Then God help you," was the chill reply.

As the *Delight* sailed past the *Pequod,* her captain suddenly noticed the coffin lifebuoy hanging from the back of the ship. "A strange lifebuoy you have," he said. "If you continue to hunt Moby Dick, you may yet have to turn it into a canoe coffin again."

Alone once more on the ocean, Ahab became very quiet. Starbuck was the only member of the crew brave enough to approach the captain now.

The First Officer slowly walked onto the quarter deck. Ahab was looking out to sea, and could not have seen him approach. Yet he must

"Here in this hand I hold his death."

have felt Starbuck's presence. He started to talk. For the moment at least, Ahab had stopped his mad ranting. He was in a reflective mood.

"Mr. Starbuck," he said, "there's a mild wind blowing. It reminds me of the day I caught and killed my first whale. I was a boy harpooner of eighteen years."

Starbuck saw a tear forming in Ahab's eye.

"That was forty years ago," continued Ahab. "Forty years have I braved the perils of the pitiless oceans. Forty years facing the horrors of the deep. I have spent but three of those forty years ashore."

"Forty years is a long time to be at sea, Captain," replied Starbuck.

"When I think of my life," continued Ahab, "I think of the solitude, the salted food and fish, and moldy bread. I think of the young wife I married and then left the very next day, to sail for Cape Horn. She is still alive, yet she has been my 'widow' for those forty years. Oceans have separated us for most of our lives. But we have a son.

"What an old fool I have been. Why have I spent my life in pursuit of whales? Am I any richer for it? No! Nothing have I gained from it but a lost leg, and a hatred of the whale that stole it. But I cannot fight that hatred. I must meet that White Whale. Revenge must be mine. Ahab will chase that monster to its death!"

Starbuck now moved right beside the captain. "Why should you bother any more with the White Whale?" he asked. "Leave the beast. Turn the ship around and take us all back to Nantucket. Your wife will be waiting for you. The fire will be roaring in the Spouter Inn. Take that seat by the fireplace and tell the youngsters and your son about your great travels and brave deeds. Come on, Captain, it's not too late. Turn the ship around. Sail for home!"

But Ahab was not listening now. He was staring up into the topsails to where Fedallah was sitting, silent as ever. At that moment Captain Ahab's nostrils had picked up a scent.

They say that whalers who have spent years at sea can smell when a whale is close. And Ahab's nose was as sharp as Fedallah's prophesies. Slowly, so very slowly, he saw Fedallah raise his right arm and point out to sea. He knew immediately what Fedallah had seen.

"All hands on deck!" he screamed. "All

"Come on, Captain, it's not too late."

hands on deck! Mastheaders! What d'you see?"

The watchmen at the mastheads all replied that they could see nothing.

"Wash your eyes out!" shouted Ahab. "Fedallah's not blind. He's seen something. Turn the ship about, helmsman."

The *Pequod* turned in the direction of Fedallah's pointing arm, now jabbing out to the westward horizon.

Then came a call from one of the men at the masthead. "There she blows! There she blows! She's got a snowy hump!"

The second masthead watcher now cried out. "It has a great forehead with wrinkles."

The third watcher went one further. "It's Moby Dick!" he shouted at the top of his voice.

Chapter 20
The Chase Begins

Fired by the cries from aloft, all the crew rushed to the side of the ship to see the infamous whale. The *Pequod* was closer to it now. The creature was less than a mile away. He was a giant and they could see him rolling majestically through the seas, regularly jetting his spout into the air.

A look of shock dawned on each man's face. They were sure this was the same beast that they had seen in the Atlantic. Either the whale had been following their journey, or the ship had been following the whale.

"There she blows!" cried Ahab again. "Stand by the boats! Bring the ship around! Steady now. Steady."

"Boats ready, Captain," called out a crewman, manning the boat cranes.

Ahab turned to Starbuck. "You stay behind," he said. "Take charge of the ship. This is my kill. Moby Dick is mine. Now, launch the boats!"

The creature was less than a mile away.

The three whaleboats were launched, one led by Stubb with Tashtego, the second with Flask and Daggoo and the third with Fedallah, Queequeg and Captain Ahab, his harpoon already attached to the long coil of rope at the bottom of the front of the vessel.

A death-glimmer lit up Fedallah's sunken eyes.

The whaleboats, carrying all sail, speeded the hunters towards their prey. The closer they sailed to the beast, the flatter and calmer the sea became. Soon it had become as flat as a mill pond.

The hunters came so close to the whale that they could see his entire dazzling white hump sliding along through the sea. The creature seemed totally unaware of their presence.

At last, Captain Ahab was just a few yards from his prey. He could clearly see the large wrinkles, the slightly projecting head and the glistening white shadows on Moby Dick's broad, milky-white forehead. And still sticking out of his side were two harpoons that had hit the beast in previous attacks.

Moby Dick swam on, still hiding most of the terrors of the awesome size of his submerged trunk. Was it possible that the whale still hadn't felt the presence of his great enemy, so close behind him? Or was Moby Dick playing tricks on his would-be killer?

Before Ahab could throw the harpoon, the whale arched his body, flipped his monstrous tail and reared up into the air. For a moment the whole of the gigantic creature could be seen. Moby Dick, as had been guessed by those that had seen him before, must have weighed around ninety tons. He looked at least ninety feet in length, too.

The great whale had finally revealed his true power and grace. He blew loudly from his blow-hole in triumph and then dived, slipping gracefully beneath the flat ocean surface.

The three whaleboats reached the spot where Moby Dick had vanished and stopped. All was complete and utter silence. No one spoke. Hearts were pumping. How long would the whale stay submerged?

Ahab peered into the clear ocean depths beneath his boat; staring as deep as his eyes could manage. Suddenly, he saw a tiny white spot far below. It was getting bigger all the time. Now Ahab saw two long crooked rows of white, glistening teeth.

His heart missed a beat. Moby Dick was

The whale reared up into the air.

surfacing again. He was right below them and rising at speed. What he had seen was Moby Dick's yawning mouth.

"Steer away!" screamed Ahab, waiting for the beast to crash through the bottom of the boat. "The devil knew we were here all along!"

Ahab just had time to rise to his feet, steady his whalebone leg and grasp his harpoon. But Moby Dick, with the terrifying intelligence recognized by all who had ever seen him, adjusted his upward charge to match the boat's movement.

As he broke through the surface, his enormous mouth, filled with more than twenty teeth, opened wide and caught the front of the boat in a vice-like grip. The crew looked on in absolute horror as the lower jaw of the whale arched high into the air. Huge pearl-white teeth hovered just inches above Ahab's head.

The whale clamped his jaws shut, barely missing Ahab and the rest of the crew. Then he shook the boat as a cat might shake the smallest mouse. The oarsmen tumbled over each other to escape to the back of the boat. Ahab just stood where he was and stared in awe, holding his harpoon in a frozen, immoveable hand. Fedallah remained motionless and gazed at the creature.

With terror washing over the boat from front to back, the whale started to play with the doomed vessel in a devilish fashion, tossing it this way and that as he chose. There was nothing the two other boats could do. If they threw their harpoons, they ran the risk of hitting Ahab or one of his crew, as well as the whale.

Ahab, recovering his wits at last, was furious as the tantalizing closeness of his foe. He struck out with his harpoon, but only succeeded in scratching Moby Dick. The whale replied by opening his jaws and freeing the boat. But only for the shortest moment. His jaws snapped shut once more, and broke the boat in two.

Ahab and Queequeg were sent flying into the air, before finally plunging into the sea and joining the rest of the crew, now without a boat beneath them. The whale, having destroyed his enemy's boat, now circled the survivors, lashing his tail and churning the water in his vengeful wake. The sight of the splintered boat seemed to madden him.

Ahab was too crippled to swim, but he could keep afloat with the help of Queequeg and

Terror washed over the boat.

Fedallah. Now the whale began to swim in ever-decreasing circles. Moby Dick was closing in for the kill.

Ahab suddenly saw the *Pequod* moving closer to them. He shouted out to Starbuck, who was watching the scene from the ship. "Sail towards the whale. Drive the monster off!"

The ship turned and, yard by yard, moved forward. At last it came between the attacker and its intended victims.

Moby Dick took one sullen look at the ship, sent out a powerful jet of air and steam from his blow-hole, and swam off. At last, the other boats moved in to rescue the survivors.

Chapter 21
Moby Dick Reappears

Ahab, with bloodshot, blinded eyes and sea salt caked in his wrinkles, was finally dragged into Stubb's boat. He lay slumped at its bottom, crushed and defeated. He should have been dead but it seemed that thoughts of vengeance against Moby Dick kept him from death's door. Or perhaps it was Fedallah's prophecy. Fedallah, along with Queequeg, had also been saved.

For a while, Ahab lay unmoving at the bottom of the boat. At last, he groaned and raised himself on one elbow. "Where's my harpoon?" he asked, as if nothing else mattered in life.

"We have it, Captain," replied Stubb. "We rescued it from the smashed boat."

"Are any of my men missing?" asked Ahab.

"All safe," said Stubb.

"Good," sighed Ahab. "Now, help me up. I want to see where that monster has got to."

Moby Dick was now some way in the distance. Ahab cursed when he saw the creature. His blood was up again. "To your oars! To your oars! We'll have the beast yet."

The men reluctantly returned to their oars. But now there were two oarsmen to each oar. On whaling operations, it was expected that rescued men would double up on the oars of the rescue boat.

Stubb's boat was now moving twice as fast. But as soon as they got close to Moby Dick, the whale swiftly moved out of harpoon distance. It was getting late in the afternoon, and Ahab finally called off the hunt. Everyone returned to the *Pequod.*

Four men were immediately sent up to the masthead, to watch Moby Dick's movements. Meanwhile, Ahab and Starbuck went to see the remains of the shattered whaleboat. The two halves of the boat had been dragged onto the quarter deck.

"It's an ill omen," said Starbuck.

"Omen my foot!" cried Ahab. "The whale will pay for this."

That evening there was an argument among the crew about who had won Ahab's bag of gold by sighting the White Whale first. Ahab

"To your oars! To your oars!"

settled the matter when he appeared on deck after resting for a while.

"The bag is mine," he said. "I smelt him long before any or you saw him. The prize is mine!"

The day was nearly done, and the sun was sinking below the horizon. Soon it was almost dark, but the lookouts were ordered to stay at the mastheads.

Ahab called up to the men, "Aloft there, men. D'ye see him? Sing out for every time you see his spout, even if he spouts a hundred times."

"Still traveling in the same direction, I think," was the reply from above. "But we can't see him any more. It's too dark out there."

Ahab called for some of the sails to be lowered to slow the speed of the ship. "We don't want to run over him in the night. I want my revenge in daylight. He won't have gone far. He's probably hove-to for a rest before the battle begins again."

With that, he settled his bone leg into its pivot, adjusted his slouching hat and stared out to sea. He didn't move until morning.

At daybreak, there was no sign of Moby Dick. Ahab ordered full speed again. The ship tore on, leaving a deep sea valley behind it.

"By my heart," rambled Ahab, "it feels good to be on the chase again. This ship and I are two brave fellows. Ha! Ha! My spine is as strong as a ship's keel. My eyes better than any number of men on the masthead. Moby Dick won't be far ahead now."

And he wasn't.

"There she blows!" was the cry from the masthead. "There she blows!"

"Aye, aye!" yelled Ahab. "I knew it. The whale can't escape me. I'm as mad as the beast itself. And I'll be the victor at day's end. Look to your life, Moby Dick. Ahab and his deadly harpoon are on your tail."

Moby Dick watched the boats being prepared for launch. Then he dived and vanished for several minutes.

The crews of the three boats, waiting to be dropped into the ocean, shivered in their boots. What had happened the day before was still etched in their memories. Where and when would Moby Dick surface again?

Suddenly, there was a great explosion of white water some way off. Moby Dick burst from the smooth surface of the ocean and flew heavenwards, his tail twisting dramatically. It was almost as if the creature had learned to fly and was showing off his powers to the enemy. For a terrifying moment, the figure of the whale, all his ninety tons or more, was in silhouette against the pale blue sky.

It was the first time that some of the crew of the *Pequod* had seen Moby Dick in his complete, awesome majesty.

"There he flies!" cried everyone. "There he flies!"

"That's the last time you fly," shouted Ahab. "The hour and the harpoon have come. Launch the boats."

The magnificent monster of the deep hung in the air for what seemed an eternity. Finally, the massive body plunged back to the water, sending up a huge plume of spray. Moby Dick vanished again.

Ahab grabbed his harpoon as three boats were dropped into the water. Daggoo was in Flask's boat, Tashtego with Stubb's and Ahab led the third boat with Queequeg and Fedallah. Starbuck stayed aboard the *Pequod*. "Don't let Moby Dick come between the ship and us again," ordered Ahab.

It was as if Moby Dick had heard him. The whale suddenly reappeared. And, as if to strike terror into the hearts of the boatmen, he was

Moby Dick flew heavenwards.

surfing at furious speed straight towards them. There was no doubting it now. Moby Dick was coming for the three crews.

Chapter 22
The Battle Continues

Ahab's boat was in the middle of the three. The captain, harpoon in hand, stood up, raised his hat and cheered on his men. "Be brave, lads," he roared. "We'll meet him head on. Stand firm!"

The whale, churning the waters as he gained speed, raced closer to the boats. He showed no fear of the waiting harpooners.

Ahab's boat led the attack as the whale came within reach. The captain's harpoon flew fast and true, as did Queequeg's. They both struck and held firm in Moby Dick's massive body. Then two more from the other boats also hit their target.

The assault slowed the whale's charge, but only for a few moments. Then he came charging straight at them again with his mouth wide open, lashing them with his powerful tail. The furious beast ignored the jagged irons in his sides as he set about destroying his attackers.

He came charging straight at them again.

For a moment, it seemed Ahab and his men might win the battle this time. But the real battle for the harpooners was now to ensure that the rope lines linking them with their harpoons didn't get too crossed.

The more pain Moby Dick felt, the more he zigzagged among the boats, desperate to free himself. The long lines became more and more entangled.

Ahab saw the danger and pulled in the slack. The other harpooners did the same. Each one was hoping that the whale would tire with the force of three boats, four harpoons and three crews pulling against it.

It only infuriated Moby Dick more. He twisted and corkscrewed through the raging white water and forced his attackers to think again. Each man reached for his knife. There was no alternative. If they hung on, the whale would drag them to a watery grave. They had to cut the lines to save themselves.

Before the whalers could do so, the whale twisted and turned one last time, and made a dash between the mass of tangled lines. Moby Dick's frantic charge freed two of the harpoons and tied the boats of Stubb and Flask in knots. The boats were dragged beneath the whale's massive tail, which immediately descended, dashing them to pieces.

The two crews found themselves in the water, each man shouting for help. Flask, terrified that the whale would return, was swimming with his legs tucked up beneath him to avoid losing his limbs to a passing shark.

Ahab ordered his crew to go to the rescue. But even as he gave the order, his boat seemed lifted up towards heaven by some invisible ropes. The White Whale had turned, dived and surfaced right beneath the boat, sending it skywards. The boat overturned in the air and crashed to the surface, landing upside down.

Ahab, Queequeg and the oarsmen swam out from beneath it as it began to sink. They watched as Moby Dick swam away, with two harpoons still piercing his side and a tangle of ropes behind him.

Soon the whale stopped and appeared to look back. He flashed his tail triumphantly several times, seemingly pleased with his work. Then he turned and silently swam away.

At the same moment, the *Pequod* came to the rescue. Soaking wet, terrified and shaking uncontrollably, the survivors clambered

They watched as Moby Dick swam away.

aboard. Ahab must have come closest to death. Yet now he was now standing on deck, leaning on Starbuck. His whalebone leg had been snapped off, leaving just one sharp splinter to stand on.

"That devil's nipped me again. There's not many who can boast losing the same leg twice," muttered Ahab, before shouting up to the mast-head to see if the whale could still be seen.

"Dead ahead, sir," was the reply.

"Raise all sail!" ordered Ahab. "We don't want to lose the beast now. And bring out the spare boats and rig them."

The *Pequod* had three spare boats for emergencies. They were brought onto the deck and hung on the launching cranes, ready to be dropped into the ocean.

It was a miracle that Moby Dick hadn't killed everyone involved in the latest battle with him. But all had cuts, sprains and scars to remember it by.

Just then, the captain looked around anxiously. "Where's Fedallah?"

No one said a word. Ahab asked again if anyone had seen him.

A sailor aboard Stubb's boat finally spoke. "I saw him," said the man. "He was caught by a harpoon line from your boat. He might have been dragged under."

"Was it my line? Could it have been my line?" wondered Ahab, his face suddenly going quite white. "There's a death-knell in those words. A death-knell for me, perhaps."

Ahab then became very agitated. "Come on men. Prepare the boats. I'll slay that whale if I have to go round the world ten times. And my trusty harpoon is in its side now, and I want it back."

Starbuck couldn't believe what he was hearing. "Good grief, Captain," he cried. "You'll never capture that whale even if he has fifty harpoons in his side. This is madness! You've chased the creature for two days, lost most of your whaleboats and lost your leg again. Now it seems that Fedallah is lost, too. Shall we keep chasing the beast until we are all dead? Shall we all be dragged to the bottom of the ocean, just for the sake of one whale?"

Ahab started to ramble like a madman again. "Our futures are all written already. Ahab may lose a leg, but he can have a hundred legs if necessary. And tomorrow I will chase the whale once more. After that, he will never rise again. He is about to spout his last."

The captain retired to his cabin. There, he began to think about Fedallah's riddle. He remembered the words.

"I cannot tell you how you'll die, but you will not die before you see two coffins on the sea. I will die before you. My death will show you the way. You will see me again after I die, and beware a piece of old rope."

Ahab shivered. Fedallah had already gone before him. But he was puzzled. "If Fedallah has gone already, how can I see him again?" he

"This is madness!"

wondered. "Now there's a riddle to be puzzled out. Like a hawk's beak it's pecking at my brain. I'll solve it though."

As dusk descended, the White Whale was still in sight. Few of the crew slept that night. They were too busy rigging the spare boats and getting ready for the next day.

Few missed the sounds of the night that echoed 'til dawn – the noise of the carpenter making the captain a new leg, the haunting cry of a lost sea bird, and the coffin lifebuoy gently tapping on the back rail of the ship.

Chapter 23
The Third Day

The morning of the third day dawned fair and fresh. The single night watchman at the foremast now found himself joined by a small army of watchers, three to each of the three masts and many others spread out on the spars.

"Do you see him?" hollered Ahab, fixing on his new leg.

The whale was not in sight. A few minutes later, the captain called again. "Aloft there! What do you see?"

Again the answer was nothing. Noon came and went, and there was still no sign of Moby Dick.

"The cursed whale," muttered the captain. "We've overtaken him in the night. Aye, he's chasing me now. Not I, him. I know it, the cunning devil."

Ahab ordered the ship to turn around and sail back for a while. Starbuck was dismayed. As far as he was concerned, Ahab had set a course directly for Moby Dick's open jaw. He turned to Stubb. "My bones," he said, "are already feeling damp. I doubt any of us will be alive at the end of this day."

Ahab now slowly climbed into the rigging and took his place at the forward masthead. He looked around and saw nothing moving at all on the wide ocean. He stayed up in the rigging all day.

The sun was beginning to set when, at last, he saw a familiar sight. In the distance, a whale was spouting. It could only be Moby Dick.

"Face to face, I meet him for a third time in as many days," shouted Ahab. "Prepare the boats!"

Before Ahab descended to the deck, he turned and looked out over the ocean. I was close enough to hear his softly spoken words.

"The sea has been my friend all my life," he murmured. "It is an old and familiar sight. It still seems the same as when I first saw it as a boy, looking out from the sand hills of Nantucket. What hopes I had then. Now, I am reduced to chasing a whale that seems determined to kill me. One of us will die today, that's for sure."

What he was saying must have reminded

It could only be Moby Dick.

him of Fedallah's words again, for after a moment, he continued to speak.

"I'm sure Fedallah said he would go before me," he muttered, "but that I would see him again before I die. I will need to have eyes at the bottom of the sea if I am to see Fedallah again. And all night I have been sailing away from where he sank to the bottom. Fedallah must have got it wrong."

Ahab then hugged the mast. "Goodbye old masthead," he said sadly. "We'll talk again tomorrow. For sure, I will return. My life is not quite done yet. There is work to do, revenge to take, a whale to die. Some men die at the coming in of a tide. Others die when it is going out. I know not yet when I will die. But, by the gods, I'm sure by tomorrow Moby Dick will be at his final anchor, hanging dead from the side of my ship."

The captain then climbed down to the deck and clambered into his boat. "Lower the boats!" he shouted.

Ahab and his crew, including myself replacing Fedallah, and the other two boats were lowered onto the water. Then something very strange happened. All three boats were quickly surrounded by sharks. Ahab ignored them, even when one maliciously snapped at the blades of the oars.

Starbuck was watching. "The man is mad," he mused to himself. "Yet what bravery! What man would launch a boat into the middle of a school of angry sharks, and then go in search of an even more dangerous enemy."

The boats had not gone very far when there was a signal from the forward masthead. The watcher was pointing.

Ahab saw the spot. The spouting devil was there, just below the surface, he was sure of it. "Beast of the sea," he cried, "I have no fear of you. No two coffins can appear for me today. And for sure, Fedallah will not come back to life. And what rope should I be wary of? It's nonsense!"

Suddenly, the waters around the boats started to swell in broad circles. The sharks had moved away and something far larger was now circling them, just out of the reach of any harpoon.

Moby Dick was back.

Surrounded by sharks.

Chapter 24
The Final Assault

The whale circled our boats as we waited, breathless with fear, for him to emerge. Then suddenly, he burst from the depths, bedraggled with trailing ropes and with the harpoons still in his side.

Once more Moby Dick hung in the air for a moment, before plunging back to the surface. Plumes of water shot fifty feet above the ocean's surface.

"Give way! Give way! He is mine!" roared Ahab, ordering his oarsmen to give chase.

The captain stood, harpoon in hand, ready for the attack that he knew must be coming.

Moby Dick had swum a little way off, before turning to face his enemy. Now, moving forward, he gained speed. Soon he was racing across the water, his tail lashing furiously. He smashed head-on into Flask and Stubb's boats, sending them and their crews tumbling into the water again. Ahab's boat was untouched.

He smashed head-on into Flask and Stubb's boats.

It was as if the whale wanted to remove the lesser contestants from the field of battle before the final assault. Moby Dick wanted Ahab. So did the sharks that had gathered again.

"Will these sharks feast on me or Moby Dick?" wondered Ahab.

At last, the whale began to swim at speed towards Ahab and his boat. The captain rose again, a harpoon in his hand, and waited. The moment came. Ahab released the harpoon. It struck Moby Dick a fierce blow in the side. Instantly, the whale writhed in agony and turned his body against the boat.

Ahab was ready. He gripped he sides of the boat with all his strength. He wasn't going to be thrown into the water a third day running. The crew and myself were not so prepared. We were all thrown out. Several of my shipmates quickly vanished beneath the waves.

Bobbing up and down in the water, I saw Ahab take two oars himself and turn the boat towards the whale again. Just then, the *Pequod* emerged from the mists that were now settling over the battleground. The ship now stood between Moby Dick and the captain's whale-boat.

The Final Assault

The great whale roared in anger and charged the *Pequod*, hitting it amidships with an unearthly crash. Timbers shattered, crewmen were flung to the decks and a great, gaping hole appeared in the ship's hull. Water began to pour in.

Ahab was now looking towards the back of the doomed ship which would soon take most of his crew to their graves. He caught sight of Queequeg's coffin, still hanging there.

"Queequeg's coffin!" he cried. "That's the first coffin. And the ship is the second. The ship is becoming a coffin too. Two coffins!"

But still Ahab couldn't bring himself to believe Fedallah's prophecy. Besides, how was he going to see Fedallah again? The man was dead – drowned and gone to the bottom of the sea.

Just then, Moby Dick dived beneath the sinking ship, causing it to heel over to one side before rolling back. The move created a wave which loosened what looked like a bundle of rags caught on the keel.

But it wasn't rags. It was Fedallah's body which floated out onto the surface of the water again.

Ahab saw it and cursed. "So you spoke the

"Queequeg's coffin!"

truth, Fedallah. I have seen you again. Yet, there's still hope for me. Beware the rope, you said. What rope?"

Moby Dick had now stopped some distance away, and was watching Ahab. Ahab knew that somehow the monster whale had already beaten him. But he rallied his spirits.

"Oh Moby Dick, thou all-destroying and unconquerable whale, to the last I battle with you. We are now connected by harpoon and line, and you may tow me to my death. But, cursed whale, I have one last harpoon to stop you yet."

Moby Dick charged again, with terrifying speed. It was as if he knew his lifeblood was failing him and soon he would die. Ahab was waiting. At last his moment came. His arched back and outstretched arm shot forward. Another harpoon flew straight and fast.

"Take that!" roared the captain.

The harpoon, and the curse, hit home. The harpoon shaft sank up to its hilt in Moby Dick's underbelly. "I have him at last" Ahab shouted gleefully.

Moby Dick spun into the air, twisting and turning in his death throes. The mortally wounded whale slowly rolled over and dived beneath the waves.

"To the devil of the deep with you!" laughed Ahab. "You'll sleep with my ship and drowned crew tonight."

The captain was so overjoyed by his victory that he failed to see that the rope line connecting him and his boat to the whale was running out. He looked down just in time to see the last few loops of rope vanishing over the side of the boat. One of the loops suddenly caught on an oar and flew up into the air. Like a perfect noose, it descended around Ahab's neck.

The captain spoke his last words, as his hands clutched at his neck. "The rope! Fedallah's rope!"

His hands clutched at his neck.

Then he said no more. He was whipped from the whaleboat and into the air, before crashing back into the sea. Moby Dick dived for the last time and dragged Captain Ahab to a lonely grave beneath the Pacific Ocean.

I saw that the hull of the *Pequod* had almost vanished below the surface. Only the mast-heads were still above the water level. At the top of them, watchmen cried out in horror. They had no chance of escaping. If they didn't drown, the sharks would get them.

The next moment, the *Pequod* vanished completely.

Chapter 25
Survival

After the *Pequod* sank, taking most of the crew with her, I held onto what remained of Stubb's whaling boat. But even that boat fell to pieces almost immediately.

I was drawn into a powerful vortex of water, created as the *Pequod* sank deeper and deeper in another world. Round and round I went. I tried to swim away, but the currents were too powerful. I was exhausted and knew I was about to join the rest of the luckless crew.

Suddenly, I was hit by something that burst to the surface right beside me. It was Queequeg's lifebuoy coffin. It must have broken away from the stern of the *Pequod* which was now way beneath me. I grabbed one of the thirty ropes hanging from it and clambered aboard. It proved to be a fine lifebuoy.

That coffin was my home for the next two

It proved to be a fine lifebuoy.

weeks. I managed to remove its lid, and slip inside. Fortunately for me, it still held the remains of the food and water that Queequeg had ordered to be placed inside it, when he thought he was dying.

One of his harpoons was also inside the coffin, as well as a paddle. I used the harpoon to fend off sharks and even caught some fish with it. The paddle helped me travel a little faster across the ocean, though I knew not where I was going.

The canoe coffin stayed afloat, even when the seas became rough and stormy. Mr. Able, the ship's carpenter, had made the *Pequod's* lifebuoy well.

On the fourteenth day, I saw a sail in the distance. I desperately waved and shouted, and finally attracted the ship's attention. The ship was the *Rachel* still criss-crossing the ocean in search of the captain's son.

The captain and crew of the *Rachel* were kind enough to take me aboard, even though Ahab had refused to help them find the captain's son. They never did find the missing boy, but at least they had rescued me – the last survivor of the fearsome battle between Captain Ahab and Moby Dick.

Survival

Somehow I lived to tell the tale of man against monster, and sail the high seas for many a long year to come. For that, I'll be forever grateful.

The End

Pride and Prejudice

By Jane Austen

A new adaptation by Archie Oliver

Jane Austen's romantic masterpiece!
The love match between the free-spirited
Elizabeth Bennet and the fiercely proud
aristocrat Fitzwilliam Darcy has captivated
readers for nearly 200 years.

The story has been made into numerous
films and television series.

Elizabeth and Darcy's love affair is played
out against a backdrop of some of literature's most enduring characters . . .
Elizabeth Bennet's mother, desperate to
find husbands for her five daughters; the
long-suffering Mr. Bennet; the gallant
Mr. Bingley and his jealous sister Caroline;
the haughty Lady Catherine de Bourgh
and the pompous Reverend William
Collins.
Jane Austen's characters are as real today
as they were when she first penned her
best-selling novel.

Great Expectations
By Charles Dickens

A new adaptation by Archie Oliver

Young Pip is shocked when he meets an escaped convict in a lonely churchyard. It's a terrifying experience that changes his life forever.

Helped by a mysterious benefactor, the orphan boy grows up to become a wealthy gentleman . . . yet memories of that day in the churchyard return to haunt him.

The story of Pip's life and loves, set against the violent nineteenth century underworld, introduces some of Charles Dickens' most famous characters . . . the convict Magwitch, the tragic Miss Haversham, the kindly Mr. Joe, the pompous Uncle Pumblechook, the wily lawyer, Mr. Jaggers, and the murderous Orlick.

The Three Musketeers
By Alexandre Dumas

A new adaptation by Archie Oliver

All for one, one for all . . . with their famous call to action, young D'Artagnan and the three musketeers, Athos, Porthos and Aramis, blaze a riotous trail for good against evil.

The four Frenchmen will fight anyone who crosses their path, whether it's the Cardinal de Richelieu's brutal guards, the dangerous Count de Rochefort, the venomous spy Milady or even the invading English army.

Alexandre Dumas' classic tale of seventeenth century political intrigue, espionage, romance and spectacular action is an adventure story without equal.

Journey to the Centre of the Earth

By Jules Verne

A new adaptation by Archie Oliver

"We are about to begin an extraordinary journey," said Professor Lidenbrock, "nothing less than an expedition to the center of the earth!"

With those words the Professor, his nephew Axel and their guide Hans climbed down into an extinct volcano crater, and began an amazing subterranean odyssey.

Living examples of extinct monsters, an underground ocean and a terrifying journey on the back of an erupting volcano are all part of Jules Verne's most extraordinary epic of science fiction.

Frankenstein

By Mary Shelley

A new adaptation by Archie Oliver

When scientist Victor Frankenstein creates a human being from stolen body parts, he instantly hates the ugly monster he has brought into the world.

The creature desperately seeks the love of its master, but is rejected. Frankenstein's monster, now friendless and unloved, sets out to destroy its creator, his family and friends.

Frankenstein is one of the most famous horror stories ever told, and has brought a chill of fear to generations of readers around the world.

Pollyanna

By Eleanor Hodgman Porter

A new adaptation by Archie Oliver

It takes a woman's hand and heart, or a child's presence, to make a home.

When the orphan Pollyanna is sent to live with her lonely aunt, she touches the lives of all those she meets. With her bright and cheerful manner she brings her new home, the Harrington homestead, to life.

The eleven-year-old girl creates happiness with her special "game", showing people that there is always something to be glad about, however bad things may seem.

But can Pollyanna teach her aunt the true magic of the game?

Tom Sawyer
By Mark Twain

A new adaptation by Archie Oliver

There never was a more mischievous boy than Tom Sawyer. And never was there a more famous show-off, adventurer and prankster on the Mississippi river!

Follow the adventures of Tom as he sails through one scrape after another. Somehow he is always the hero of his own story, especially when his free-spirited sidekick, Huckleberry Finn, is with him.

Mark Twain's famous tale, set against a backdrop of nineteenth century life on the Mississippi, is a classic of American literature.

The Wind in the Willows

by Kenneth Grahame

A new adaption by Archie Oliver

Life becomes one great adventure for Mole when he meets his new riverside friends, Water Rat, Badger and Toad.

Mole is half-drowned by young Ratty's love of messing about in boats, becomes lost in the woods, and is astonished to find that gentleman Toad has suddenly become a speed-mad convict! He goes on to fight bravely with Badger against the wily weasels and stoats, and helps bring peace to the Wild Wood.

Generations of young readers had delighted in Kenneth Grahame's enchanting animal tales from the riverbank.

The Time Machine

By H.G. Wells

In 1890 a Victorian scientist tells his friends
he has built a Time Machine that will take
him far into the future. His friends don't
believe him. But then the man vanishes.
The Time Traveler eventually returns to
tell his friends that he has journeyed
nearly a million years into the future
to the year 802,701.

He reveals how he discovers a new race of
human beings called the Eloi. They seem to
enjoy a perfect life of leisure and enjoyment.
But the nightmarish truth only emerges
when the Time Traveler meets the Morlocks,
a dread underworld race of creatures.

H.G. Wells' vision of the future and the Time
Traveler's extraordinary adventures create a
terrifying masterpiece of science
fiction. *Titles in this series*

Treasure Island

By Robert Louis Stevenson

The one-legged Long John Silver,
treacherous Captain Billy Bones, wicked
Black Dog and the terrifying Blind Pew …
they were the cruelest and most frightening
pirates ever to sail the high seas.
They all dreamed of finding Captain Flint's
buried treasure.

But it was young Jim Hawkins, just 14 years
old, who found Flint's map of Treasure
Island. Could he and his friends outwit those
bloodthirsty pirates? And what secrets lay
with Ben Gunn, the wild man of the island?

Robert Louis Stevenson's classic story,
which has thrilled generations of younger
readers, is the most famous pirate
adventure of them all.

20,000 Leagues Under the Sea

By Jules Verne

In 1866 newspapers across the planet are full of stories about a terrifying creature haunting the world's oceans.

Professor Pierre Aronnax, along with his servant Conseil and the master harpooner Ned Land, join the global hunt for the monster. They discover that the beast is actually the *Nautilus*, a futuristic submarine designed by the mysterious Captain Nemo.

Captured and imprisoned aboard the *Nautilus*, the Professor and his companions begin an extraordinary journey ... one that reveals the deepest secrets of both the world's oceans and the terrifying Captain Nemo.

Black Beauty

By Anna Sewell

Born on a sunlit meadow in an English village, Black Beauty has a happy upbringing and a wonderful home, with a kind and caring master. Then the beautiful young horse is sold and separated from his friends. So begins an extraordinary journey through life for Black Beauty; a journey that brings moments of triumph and joy, as well as pain, suffering, loneliness and cruelty at the hands of others.

Can Black Beauty ever find true happiness again? Will he find his way back to the peaceful meadows of his youth? Or is he condemned to live in misery for the rest of his life, like so many working horses of his time.

Black Beauty is one of the most moving animal stories ever told.

Little Women

By Louisa May Alcott

Beautiful Meg, tomboy Jo, shy Beth and head-strong Amy are the March sisters – four young ladies growing up in America during the Civil War. Their father is away in the army and the three eldest girls must work to help their mother.

Meg dreams of owning a luxurious home, while Jo wants to become a famous writer. Beth would like nothing more than to spend her days caring for her family, while Amy is determined to be a great artist.

Follow the girls' adventures as they learn many of life's lessons, through heartbreak, tears and happy times.